City of Snow

The Great Blizzard of 1888

Linda Oatman High

Illustrations by Laura Francesca Filippucci

WALKER & COMPANY

NEW YORK

It was Sunday morning,
March 11, 1888, and rain was falling,
spraying a steady tempest from heaven.

It drenched our heads
and my best dress
as Mama and Papa and I left church,
    umbrella-less.

Purple and yellow crocuses shone
in the stone gray afternoon.
Springtime would soon arrive in
the city of New York.

The windows of stores were glorious,
with mannequins wearing the springtime
    fashions
as we rushed past,
splashing and dashing through the wet
    weather,
hurrying home to a Sunday dinner
at the dismal end of winter.

It rained buckets all Sunday,
and our roof began to leak.
Our kitchen floor sopping,
I prayed while I mopped,
for the rain to stop.
Tomorrow morning was P. T. Barnum's circus expedition.
I'd been saving my money for the fifty-cent admission.

Bargaining with Mama and God,
I promised to be good
and to cheerfully complete every chore,
if only I could see Barnum's most famous tour:
"The Finest Assembly of Trained Animals Since Noah,"
the newspaper did assure.

Gazing at the rain making a lake of New York
in the fast-growing dark,
I thought perhaps Papa should build us an ark
so we'd be sure to embark
on our circus-day lark.

By nightfall the rain had turned to snow,
and gutters churned with slush.
Sleet balls plinked across our roofs,
above the house's nighttime hush,
ice clip-clopping like a hundred horses' hooves.

Howling winds rattled the windows
like careless thieves,
and the eaves wheezed,
heaving as if the house were breathing.

I slept as fitful as the wind
and woke shivering in the night.
The temperature had dipped,
and whips of coldness crept
through cracks in the plaster wall.

Quivering in my quilt,
I saw a sliver of white through my window,
pale as a pitcher of milk.

I leaped from my bed at daybreak,
and ran straight to look out my window.
What was below made my eyes ache:
the blinding white of a city of snow.

There were no roads,
no wagons hauling loads,
no ponies,
no paper,
no people,
no milk,
no meat,
no streets,
no trains on tracks,
no teams, no hacks,
no sidewalks, no paths,
no *thing* but snow.

Papa couldn't get to his job,
and our old horse, Bob,
was too hobbled and wobbly legged
to pull our carriage through the drifts to the show.

Gentle Bob stood
patiently waiting
for me to come skating
with apples and carrots
to his stable.
His dappled back rippled
as he whinnied and trembled.

I whispered in Bob's ear,
telling him not to fear.
Even though the snow was fiercely wild,
I was sure that the weather would soon turn mild.

It was only a few blocks
to Madison Square,
so I begged Papa for us to walk there.

Bundled in boots and wool,
scarves and gloves and hats,
Mama and Papa and I
ventured outside like nervous cats
but plodding like mules.

Bitten by a bitter wind
as we trudged in slow single file,
we pushed and leaned,
seeing crushed storefronts
and sparrows frozen in snow,
blown and tangled telegraph wires.

We walked and walked,
and as we trudged along,
I crossed my fingers
and hoped
that P. T. Barnum's show
would go on.

We finally arrived
at Madison Square,
happily relieved
that the circus was there.

Lions and tigers and bears,
a daring girl on a high-flying trapeze,
a clown with a red-nosed sneeze,
dancing dogs and prancing ponies,
eighty-six fabulous acts in all.

"The storm may be a great show,"
said Mister Barnum, in all his mirth,
"but I still have the greatest show on
    Earth!"

Applause scattered
within the almost-empty big top,
and all that mattered
was that the fun would never stop.

When the circus ended,
we left the red tent
and stepped, bent,
into the quick icy wind
as hats and trash whipped
from the wind's wicked lash.

Our faces glazed crystal,
we battled the blizzard,
which was like a wild animal
rattling a cage,
attacking and fighting
all in a rage.

The trolleys and trains
could not move,
and passengers were rescued,
their faces white-blue.

My lungs squeezed,
and I could hardly breathe,
as we hiked slowly
toward home.

We huddled by the stove
and peeled off clothes that had froze.
We decided to make the blizzard
an occasion of celebration
by having our own
snow-party jubilation.

Eating snow ice-cream with syrup,
savoring the sweet, frosty flavor,
Mama and Papa and I made party favors
and played games with neighbors.

Some whittled, some fiddled,
some told riddles
or sang hearty old songs
to pass the time along.

All day Monday,
all Monday night,
all day Tuesday,
all Tuesday night,
the blizzard continued
its sharp, icy bite,
coating the city
with a blanket of white.

The street outside was covered
in wires from a fallen pole,
and we were running low
on milk and meat and coal.

Now the blizzard
wasn't as much fun
as it had been
when first begun.

By Wednesday
pedestrians tested their muscles,
attempting to bustle through
high piles of drifted snow.
But swiftly whirling winter winds
twirled them like little dolls.

Bulky in layers of clothing,
the walkers wore blizzard fashions
dug from trunks hunkered in attics:
dusty and musty hats and caps,
skins of cats, bears, and muskrats
all joined the scarves and mittens of
    many colors
whisked away by winter winds,
looking pretty as they littered the city.

The blizzard ended Wednesday night,
leaving behind a city of white.

It was early Thursday,
and, not caring what others said,
I wrapped a bed blanket around my head
and kept my face warm
with a rag of faded red.

We stepped through the door,
into a world that was magic:
snow making strange shapes, like waves,
and shovelers digging paths for sleighs.

Pranksters buried boots and trousers
upside down in high snowbanks,
and once I stumbled over what was only
a lonely wooden Indian that tumbled
from the porch of a cigar store.

A tunnel was dug to Lugman's Drugs,
in a drift on Sixth Avenue,
and I crawled through,
buying a blue pitcher of fizzy,
famous Blakely's Blizzard Soda.

On Friday
merchants and churches
made posters and signs,
joking about free snow
for those passing by.

There were still no deliveries of food or coal,
and we were wishing for steak and milk and eggs.
Mama made bread and kept us well fed,
and just before bed
a red-capped head appeared outside the window.

It was the milkman, Fred,
driving a horse-drawn sled,
gliding high on top of a totally frozen drift.

Fred knocked on the glass,
and we all laughed,
glad to finally have milk.

On Saturday
black rollers of steel
packed down the snow,
strong horses snorting and snuffling,
their hooves shuffling,
moving slow.

Numb from the cold,
shoveling rolled
and heavy snow,
every household
helped to load
cartfuls of snow,
to be taken below
the city roads
and dumped into the river.

Shivering,
I wished that this mess
would soon be over.

It was Sunday again,
after the blizzard that wouldn't end.
A thaw had melted most of the snow,
and gutters were churning with slush.

Icicles dripped as walkers slipped
on slick streets, greeting each other
with tired smiles.

Sunshine peeked
from the gloomy sky
for the first time in a week,
and I knew that crocuses would
once more bloom,
and we'd go back to school soon.

Splashing home from church,
my best shoes were wet,
and I knew I'd never forget
the city of snow,
the terrible Great Blizzard of 1888.

To Zach, who loves snow —L. O. H.

To my children, Anna, Bibi, and Giovanni —L. F. F.

Special thanks to Kathleen Hulser, Public Historian, the New York Historical Society.

The inspiration for the text on pages 8–9 was a headline from the Vermont Bellows Falls *Times* which read "No paths, no streets, no sidewalks, no light, no roads, no guests, no calls, no teams, no hacks, no trains, no moon, no meat, no milk, no paper, no mails, no news, no thing—but snow."

First published in the United States of America in 2004 by Walker Publishing Company, Inc.

Published simultaneously in Canada by Fitzhenry and Whiteside, Markham, Ontario L3R 4T8

For information about permission to reproduce selections from this book, write to Permissions, Walker & Company, 104 Fifth Avenue, New York, New York 10011

Library of Congress Cataloging-in-Publication Data

High, Linda Oatman.
  City of snow / Linda Oatman High ; illustrations by Laura Francesca Filippucci.
    p. cm.
  Summary: A fictionalized account, told in free-verse poems, of a young girl's experience living through the 1888 "Great Blizzard"
in New York City.
  ISBN 0-8027-8910-2 (HC) — ISBN 0-8027-8911-0 (RE)
  [1. Blizzards—New York (State) —New York—Juvenile fiction. [1. Blizzards—New York (State) —New York—Fiction. 2. New York (N.Y.) —
History—1865-1898—Fiction.] I. Filippucci, Laura, ill. II. Title.

PZ7.H543968Ci 2004
[E]—dc22

2003069058

The artist used watercolor on Arches paper, with refining in brown ink and white pastel to create the illustrations for this book.

Book design by Maura Fadden Rosenthal/Mspace*ny*

Visit Walker & Company's Web site at www.walkeryoungreaders.com

Printed in Hong Kong

2 4 6 8 10 9 7 5 3 1

Author's Note

The Blizzard of 1888 is the most famous snowstorm in the history of America. Nicknamed "the Great White Hurricane," the blizzard shut down the entire East Coast of the United States. Telephone and telegraph wires snapped, isolating the cities of New York, Philadelphia, Boston, and Washington, D.C. Two hundred ships were sunk or damaged, and more than four hundred people died.

The days leading up to the Great Blizzard were warm, with temperatures in the fifties. Because the agency that provided national weather forecasts was closed on Sundays until 5:00 p.m., the snowstorm took America by surprise. The event started as a pouring Sunday rain, then changed to heavy snow as the temperature grew colder. Fierce winds whipped, and the blizzard continued for thirty-six hours, with the snow piling higher and higher. New York City reported more than forty inches of snow, with drifts towering fifty feet high.

Men, women, children, and animals were affected by the Great Blizzard, with many stuck outside in the howling winds, struggling through the snow toward their homes. For days after the snowstorm, as New York and other cities dug out from under the snow, there was a shortage of coal and no deliveries of meat, milk, vegetables, fruits, or eggs.

In New York City, the destruction caused by the blizzard was enormous. Many travelers and residents were stranded, unable to get to their homes. Hotels overflowed, with cots crowding the lobbies. People spoke and wrote of the storm for many years, and the Great Blizzard of 1888 is still remembered as one of New York City's worst hardships. The devastation resulted from both the intense snowfall and winds and the city's lack of preparedness for such an event. The struggle to recover was a long one, and the city was changed forever.

Today, New York City is connected by hundreds of miles of subway, and all communication and electrical lines are placed underground—and of course the United States National Weather Service remains open twenty-four hours a day, every day of the year. These are just a few of the changes brought about by the Great Blizzard of 1888.

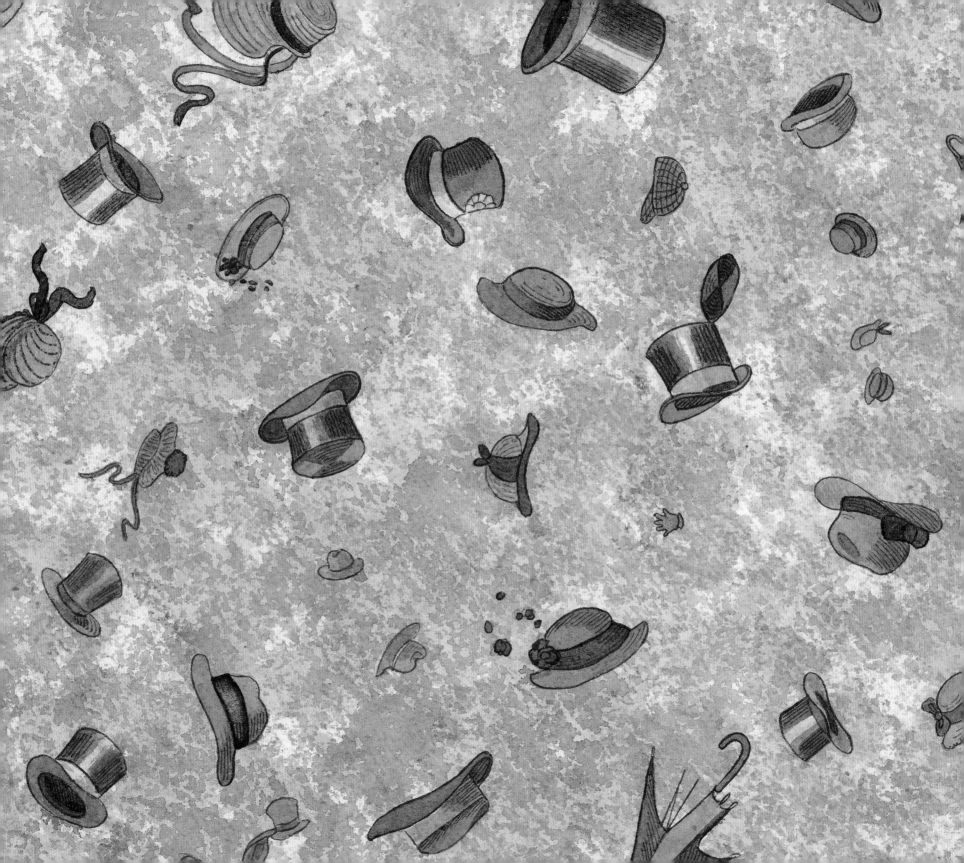